One year with
Kipper

Mick Inkpen

Hodder
Children's
Books

A division of Hachette Children's Books

In January Kipper took a picture with his new camera and made a New Year Resolution,

    'This year I will not throw any snowballs at Tiger.'

    And for a whole month he kept his promise. . .

Because the snow
did not fall until
February!

An icicle grew on
Kipper's house.
It lasted for three
weeks and grew
to 87 centimetres.

Kipper took a
photograph.

In March the wind flapped Kipper's ears.

It straightened his scarf and scruffled the daffodils on Big Hill.

Then it blew Tiger right off his feet!

Click!

This is the picture that Kipper took.

Soon the pond in the park was full of croaking and wriggling and glooping and jiggling.

'March is the froggiest month,' said Kipper.

'But April is best for catching tadpoles.'

By **May** there was blossom on the pavements thick enough to kick, and three ducklings in the park. One of them followed Tiger everywhere.

Quack!
Quack!
Click!

In June Kipper lay on his back and watched as little things with legs and wings climbed the spindly grasses and whizzed into the big, blue sky.

'There are a lot more little things with legs and wings than you would think,' thought Kipper.

The first week in **July** was hot. The second week was hotter still.

And then Boom!

BOOOM!

BOOOM!

A thunderstorm!

August was
summer holiday time.

Kipper took a parachute
ride above the sea.

'Take my
picture!'
he called
to Tiger.

In September
the bramble bushes were full
of blackberries.

The thorns were prickly.
'Ouch! Ouch!'
But the

blackberries
were delicious.

'Mmmmmmmmm!'

In October

Kipper and Tiger made a collection of autumn things.

'October is an orangey-brown sort of month,' said Tiger.

They made a face from the pumpkin which glowed in the dark.

November

came around, and twiggy branches made patterns against the misty moon.

They huffed their breath into the heavy garden air, seeing who could huff the highest.

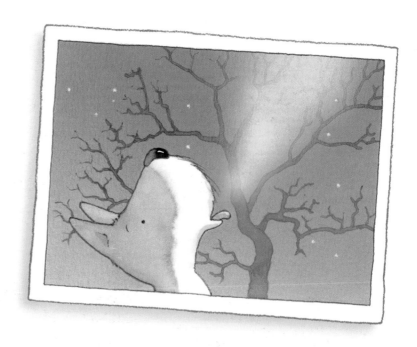

In December the days grew dark and cold.

Kipper stayed indoors making decorations and a special Christmas present for Tiger.

'I need one more photograph,' said Kipper.

So he called Tiger and got out his camera.

'Smile!'

said Kipper as he opened the front door.

But Tiger was already smiling – because it was snowing.

And because he had not forgotten about February.

Click! went Kipper's camera.

Booof!

went Tiger's snowball!

April

August

December

Christmas

day came and Kipper gave Tiger his present. 'Look at me in August!' said Kipper. But Tiger was looking at December. 'This one is the best!' he said.

First published in 2006 by Hodder Children's Books
First published in paperback in 2007

Text and illustrations copyright © Mick Inkpen 2006

Hodder Children's Books
338 Euston Road, London, NW1 3BH

Hodder Children's Books Australia
Level 17/207 Kent Street, Sydney, NSW 2000

A catalogue record of this book is available from the British Library.

ISBN: 978 0 340 91141 9
10 9 8 7 6 5 4 3

Colour reproduction by Dot Gradations Limited UK
Printed in China
Hodder Children's Books is a division of Hachette Children's Books.
An Hachette Livre UK Company